Where, Where, Where Do Mermaids Come From?

iUniverse books may be ordered through booksellers or by contacting:

iUniverse
1663 Liberty Drive
Bloomington, IN 47403
www.iuniverse.com
844-349-9409

ISBN: 978-1-6632-0727-2(sc)
ISBN: 978-1-6632-0726-5 (e)

Library of Congress Control Number: 2020915678

Print information available on the last page.

iUniverse rev. date: 10/23/2020

Where, Where, Where Do Mermaids Come From?

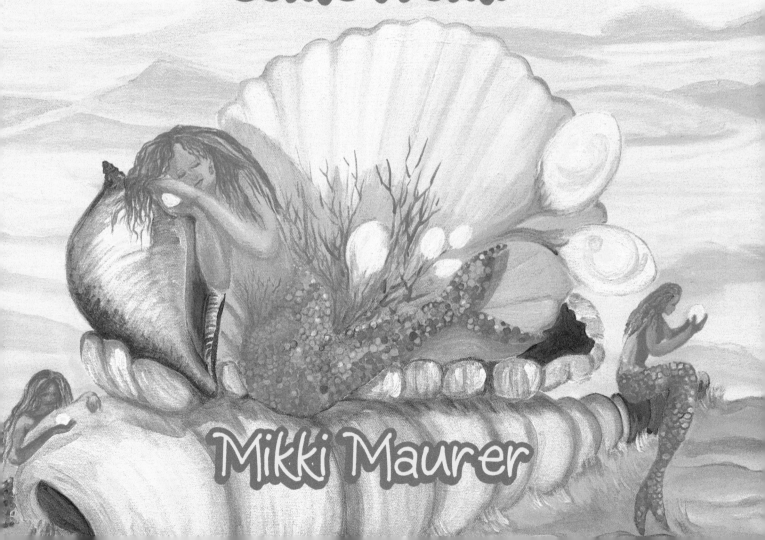

Mikki Maurer

Acknowledgments

Where, where, where do I begin to thank all the wonderful people who supported and encouraged me to complete this journey? First and foremost, I thank God for everything. Secondly, my husband, Joel, and my daughter, Meggan, for their unconditional love and support. And I thank all the following people who were constantly encouraging me to continue on and finish the book: my sisters, Colleen, Kathleen, and Eileen, whose names I loved using; and my dearest friends and colleagues, including Carolyn Tresnan, who loved teaching through storytelling.

Also thanks to Diane Engel, my reading guru; Kris Thompson, my cousin, who was the first to read a rough draft; Patricia Woodbery, my analytical councilor and confidant; and Judy Maurer, my computer expert with the patience of a saint.

Once upon a long, long, long time ago, way, way, way up in the sky, Saint Peter was standing in front of the famous Pearly Gates.

Oh my, he thought, *those pearls are very, very, very dusty*. "Ah," he hummed, "I know what to do. I must call for the angel maids. They will come and clean all the pearls."

With just a clap of his hands, a golden horn appeared on a little cloud. Saint Peter picked up the horn and, with puffy cheeks, blew, blew, blew into the horn.

The horn made a loud, loud, loud honking noise. Instantly, not one, not two, not three, but four little angel maids appeared. Each angel maid wore a little hat and a little apron and carried a feather duster and a big, big, big scrub brush.

Saint Peter spoke very softly to the angel maids. He identified them by their names: first, the oldest angel maid, Colleen; second, the funniest-looking angel maid, Maureen; third, the prettiest angel maid, Kathleen; and last but not least, the tiniest little angel maid, Eileen.

Colleen, Maureen, Kathleen, and Eileen listened carefully to Saint Peter. He instructed them to clean, clean, clean the very dusty pearls on the famous Pearly Gates.

The angel maids went right to work with their feather dusters and scrub brushes. They were making sure to go over each pearl until it was very, very, very shiny.

Suddenly, Eileen noticed one of the pearls was beginning to wobble, wobble, wobble. She flew over to the pearl just as it was falling off the gate. She tried to catch the pearl, but she could only watch as it kept falling.

The pearl fell through the sky, passing the clouds, passing the moon, passing the stars, and passing the sun. As hard as Eileen tried, she could not catch the pearl. Sadly, she watched as the pearl fell into the deep blue sea. With tiny tears, Eileen went back to cleaning the famous Pearly Gates.

As the pearl fell closer to the earth, the only thing in sight was the blue, blue, blue water. The water caught the pearl and let it sink into the deepest part of the sea. The pearl passed fish of all shapes and sizes. The pearl passed a shell flower wrapped in coral. It passed plants and seaweed until, at last, it landed softly on the bottom of the sea.

Nothing in the sea had seen anything like this before. All the fish, plants, shells, and other sea creatures were admiring the beautiful pearl. They wondered, *Where did this beauty come from?*

Day after day, the living sea protected the beautiful pearl. The fish thought, *We need more of these*. The clamshells said that they would protect the pearl from harm. The seaweed said that they would hold the pearl in their branches. Then they all agreed the sea could be the pearl's home forever.

Meanwhile, in heaven, Saint Peter was inspecting the job of the angel maids. Colleen, Maureen, Kathleen, and Eileen watched as Saint Peter examined every pearl.

Suddenly, he stopped in his tracks when he noticed that one of the pearls was missing from the famous Pearly Gates. He turned to the angel maids and asked them if they knew anything about the missing pearl. Colleen spoke first. "I know nothing about it."

Maureen said, "I know nothing about it."

Kathleen said, "I know nothing about it."

But the tiniest angel maid, Eileen, nodded and spoke very, very, very softly.

Saint Peter listened patiently while Eileen told the story of how the pearl wobbled out of the gate and fell, fell, fell out of heaven's sky. Eileen explained how she had tried to save it but had not been able to catch the beautiful pearl. After listening carefully to her, Saint Peter thanked her for trying and told her not to worry. Sadly, she went on to join the other angel maids.

Saint Peter knew then and there the beautiful pearl had found a new home.

Eileen was upset. As hard as the tiniest angel maid tried, she could not forget about the missing pearl.

Eileen thought about how she could get the pearl back to the famous Pearly Gates. She talked to the other angel maids and asked them if they had any big, big, big ideas. Colleen said, "I do."

Maureen said, "I do."

Kathleen said that she did too.

Colleen said, "Let us all go and get the pearl back from the deep, deep, deep blue sea." All the angel maids were excited to go on this adventure.

Eileen said, "Wait! I must let Saint Peter know our plan to fly down to the earth and get the pearl back from the blue, blue, blue sea."

Eileen looked for Saint Peter. He was nowhere to be found.

The angel maids were waiting for the tiniest angel maid and told her to hurry, hurry, hurry so they could go and get the pearl. Eileen decided to write a note to Saint Peter telling him the plan and then catch up with Colleen, Maureen, and Kathleen.

Together, the angel maids went flying through the sky toward the earth. They passed the clouds, they passed the sun, they passed the moon, they passed the stars, and they finally saw the deep, deep, deep blue sea. Without stopping to think about the water, the angel maids dove into the deep, deep, deep blue sea.

Saint Peter found the note that the tiniest angel maid had written and read it immediately. In a loud voice, he called out, "No!" He knew the angel maids could not swim; they knew only how to fly. Without wasting another minute, Saint Peter clapped his hands four times, making a very loud sound. At that exact moment, the angel maids began to feel very, very, very sleepy in the deep blue sea. As they gently sank to the bottom of the sea, four big, big, big clams opened their shells to catch the angel maids and keep them safe.

When Colleen, Maureen, Kathleen, and Eileen woke up, they felt very different. They were inside clamshells and could not see a thing. The clams knew the angel maids were awake, so they slowly opened their shells. To the amazement of all the sea creatures, the angel maids looked very, very, very different from when they arrived.

The angel maids could swim! Not only could they swim, but they no longer had wings, hats, aprons, or dresses. Instead, the angel maids had fish tails, fish scales, and long, long, long flowing hair. They were no longer angel maids—they had become *mermaids*!

Colleen, Maureen, Kathleen, and Eileen were very, very, very surprised at their new look. They swam around in their new world and began laughing and singing joyful songs.

The tiniest mermaid, Eileen, was wondering if Saint Peter knew what had happened and if he was happy they were safe in the sea.

Then she remembered the missing pearl.

Quickly swimming to the other mermaids, she said that they must find the pearl. They asked the fish, they asked the shell flowers, they asked the seaweed, and finally, they asked the clams if they had seen the pearl. All of them nodded to say yes, especially the clams.

The clams proceeded to open up their shells. They proudly showed the mermaids the beautiful shiny pearls that were sitting inside.

Oh my, thought the mermaids. These pearls looked exactly like the pearls on the famous Pearly Gates.

The mermaids were most curious and swam over to the pearls to look at them closely. Much to their surprise, they could see little baby mermaids starting to grow inside the pearls. All they wanted to do was help protect these beautiful pearls because one day they too would become mermaids.

Colleen, Maureen, Kathleen, and Eileen, now beautiful mermaids, looked to see if they could send Saint Peter a message way, way, way up in heaven. Just then, a very bright light appeared, and they saw the smiling face of Saint Peter.

Saint Peter knew his little mermaids were safe and happy.

From then on, Colleen, Maureen, Kathleen, and Eileen swam around with all their sea friends, collecting sea pearls and protecting them.

Now they knew it was their job to bring the sea more beautiful mermaids.

They all swam happily ever after, after, after!

(Oh, now you know where mermaids come from.)